THE HUGGLEBALL GAME

Based on the episode by Kent Redeker
Adapted by Bill Scollon
Illustrated by Premise Entertainment

ABDOPUBLISHING.COM

Reinforced library bound edition published in 2019 by Spotlight, a division of ABDO, PO Box 398166, Minneapolis, Minnesota 55439. Spotlight produces high-quality reinforced library bound editions for schools and libraries. Published by agreement with Disney Press, an imprint of Disney Book Group.

Printed in the United States of America, North Mankato, Minnesota.
042018   092018

DISNEP PRESS
New York • Los Angeles

 THIS BOOK CONTAINS
RECYCLED MATERIALS

Library of Congress Control Number: 2017960979

Publisher's Cataloging in Publication Data

Names: Scollon, Bill, author. | Redeker, Kent, author. | Premise Entertainment, illustrator.
Title: Henry Hugglemonster: The huggleball game/ by Bill Scollon and Kent Redeker; illustrated by Premise Entertainment.
Description: Minneapolis, MN : Spotlight, 2019 | Series: World of reading level pre-1
Summary: When Henry and his friends challenge the grown-ups to a game of Huggleball, Henry and Summer are named co-captains. Can they find a way to work as a team and beat the adults?
Identifiers: ISBN 9781532141799 (lib. bdg.)
Subjects: LCSH: Henry Hugglemonster (Television program)--Juvenile fiction. | Teamwork (Sports)--Juvenile fiction. | Monsters--Juvenile fiction. | Brothers and sisters--Juvenile fiction. | Readers (Primary)--Juvenile fiction.
Classification: DDC [E]--dc23

Spotlight
A Division of ABDO
abdopublishing.com

Henry is excited!
He will play Huggleball.

Summer will play, too.
So will their friends.

The kids have a team.
So do the parents.

How do you play Huggleball?

Throw the Huggleball.

Catch the Huggleball.

Run to the goal.

It is time to pick leaders.
Everyone draws a straw.

Henry draws a long straw.
Summer does, too.
They will both be leaders.

Henry has a plan.
Run fast, run hard!

Summer has a plan, too.
Dance to the goal!

Henry is excited!
His plan is first.

The game begins.
The kids get the ball.

Summer gets the ball.
Run fast, run hard!

Summer loses the ball.
The parents get the ball.

The parents score a goal!

Summer's plan is next.

Summer gets the ball.
She dances by the parents.

Summer loses the ball.
Daddo gets the ball.

Daddo scores a goal!

The parents are winning.
The kids need a new plan.

Henry has an idea.
The kids will use both plans!

Three Huggleballs are in play.
The kids catch every one.

The kids run and dance.
Summer gets to the goal.

Henry throws all three balls.
Summer catches them.

The kids win the game!

Henry and Summer worked together.
They made a great team!